Hilde Heyduck-Huth

The Strawflower

A Treasure Chest Story

Margaret K. McElderry Books
NEW YORK

Originally published by Atlantis Kinderbücher/ © 1985 Verlag Pro Juventute, Zürich,
English translation copyright © 1987 by Margaret K. McElderry Books, Macmillan Publishing Company

Margaret K. McElderry Books
Macmillan Publishing Company
866 Third Avenue
New York, NY 10022
Collier Macmillan Canada, Inc.

Composition by Linoprint Composition Co., Inc.
New York, New York
Printed by General Offset Co., Inc.
Jersey City, New Jersey
Bound by A. Horowitz and Sons
Fairfield, New Jersey

The original illustrations for *The Strawflower* are watercolor paintings.

First American Edition

Printed in the United States of America

10 9 8 7 6 5 4 3 2 1

Library of Congress Cataloging-in-Publication Data

Heyduck-Huth, Hilde.
The strawflower.

Translation of: Die Strohblume.
Summary: A strawflower passes through many hands
before a little girl finds it and puts it in her
treasure chest.
[1. Flowers—Fiction] I. Title.
PZ7.H4497St 1987   [E]   87-4254
ISBN 0-689-50435-7

The Strawflower

Many pretty flowers—pink, yellow, orange,
lilac and white—were blooming in a garden.

There was one other plant
with small pale pink blossoms and buds.

Autumn was coming.
The wind whirled leaves through the air.
All the flowers had faded
and soon the leaves covered them.
Only one plant could still be seen.
Its small pink flowers were still pretty.
They had not faded.
They were strawflowers.

Then it began to snow and some children made a snow family.
"The snowman can have my scarf around his neck
and the old cooking pot for a hat," said one child.
"I'll get some other things," said another child.

And he brought a broom, five carrots, two old shoes that didn't match,
a tin cup, a bottle, a torn apron and broken sunglasses.
"I know of something else," a third child said and ran off.
She came back soon with all the pink strawflowers
and put them into the arms of the snowlady.

When evening came, a woman saw the snow family.
She stopped and thought, "Do snow people need flowers?"
She shook her head and took the bunch of pink strawflowers
from the snowlady's arms. She carried them home
and decorated her table with them.
But next morning she shook her tablecloth out of the window.

"Why, it's raining flowers!"
said a little girl on her way to school.
She picked them up
and put them into her schoolbag,
and in the afternoon
she made herself a wreath of flowers.
She put it on her head
and went for a walk.

A man who played a flute was sitting in a doorway.
Many people passed by and threw pennies into his box.
The little girl stood still.
She liked the music, but she had no money.
Instead, she took the wreath from her head,
picked out one of the strawflowers and gave it to the man.

"What a pretty little flower," said a woman in a fur coat.
"I'd like to buy it!"
She took the flower from the flute player
and put a coin in his box.
Then she tucked the flower in a buttonhole of her coat
and went on her way.
But the strawflower slipped out and fell into the snow.

A little girl called Anna was walking with her dog.
Coco was not on a leash and suddenly he disappeared.
"Come back, Coco, come back!" Anna called.
In a minute he came into sight.
But what was he carrying in his mouth?
A pink flower, in the middle of winter! Anna was surprised.

The next day was Christmas,
and Anna decorated her Christmas tree
with stars made out of gold paper, with apples,
stuffed animals, wooden figures, gold-painted nuts,
mandarin oranges—and one pink strawflower.

When Christmas was over, Anna got out a little box.
It was her treasure chest.
She kept in it lots of pretty things she had collected:
pebbles, seashells and snail shells.
There was also a starfish that Anna had found on the beach.
She put the strawflower with the rest of the treasures.
What other things will Anna find to keep in her treasure chest?
What would you put in a treasure chest?